CLUES TO AMERICAN MUSIC

Also in this series:

Clues to American Architecture
David Fogle, Marilyn Klein, Wolcott Etienne

Clues to American Furniture
Jean Taylor Federico, Judith Curcio

Clues to American Garden Styles
David Fogle, Catherine Mahan, Chris Weeks

Clues to American Sculpture
Kathleen Sinclair Wood, Margo Pautler Klass

CLUES
to
American
Music

Monroe Levin

STARRHILL PRESS
Washington & Philadelphia

This book is for my wife Betty,
for my "co-musician" Cameron McGraw,
and for my daughters, Anne and Laurie.

Published by Starrhill Press, Inc.
P.O. Box 32342
Washington, DC 20007
(202) 686-6703

Library of Congress Cataloging-in-Publication Data

Levin, Monroe, 1923–
    Clues to American music / Monroe Levin. — 1st ed.
        p.   cm.
    Includes bibliographical references (p.   ) and index.
    ISBN 0-913515-62-0 (pbk.) : $7.95
    1. Music—United States—History and criticism.   I. Title.
ML200.L48 1992
780'.973—dc20   91-42562
                                                                         CIP

Printed in the United States of America

First edition
1 3 5 7 6 4 2

Contents

This volume was written as America prepared to celebrate the five-hundredth anniversary of its discovery by Christopher Columbus. Musically speaking, the fifty decades of New World life divide into two eras: the time before 1900 when American music of consequence was mostly indistinguishable from European styles, and the century now drawing to a close, during which American composers began to declare their independence.

Since the first nine decades of the twentieth century require our space far more than the previous forty-one, finding clues to the second era is the main purpose of this handbook. I have divided the twentieth century into three periods: 1900–1929, 1929–1968, and from 1968 on. Each includes a major war that changed the United States, and each produced a generation or more of increasingly sophisticated musicians. The pace of musical advancement in the nation during this century is truly impressive.

But the centuries before this one were by no means musically barren. There may have been no amateur composer to match what Thomas Jefferson did in architecture, no musical parallel to the Hudson River school of painting or Walt Whitman's poetry, but the potential for an identifiable American music existed even before 1800.

Listening for the pulse of that music, we set out in search of clues to its nature, keeping the lay audience in mind and a layman's glossary at hand (p. 63). Though examples of musical scores are included with the text, they are not indispensable; perhaps readers of the prose who are not able to read the music will ask a musical friend to play or sing them. In any case, the reader is not assumed to have musical knowledge or ability but only a good sense of hearing and musical curiosity.

A Word about Recordings

No musically curious person is at a complete loss today without the ability to read musical scores; a public or collegiate record library, if not a well-stocked record shop, is never far away.

The standard reference work for concert recordings of American music is *American Music Recordings: A Discography* (New York: Brooklyn College of CUNY, 1982). Although not updated since publication, its listings remain useful to those seeking an in-depth listening experience of any particular composer since 1950. Beyond the recommendations made in the text, the following list identifies the major series of recorded American music not readily available in stores (though generally found in larger libraries):

1. Composers Recordings, Inc. (issued 1954 to the present).
2. Folk Music in America, Library of Congress, Washington, D.C., fifteen discs (1977).
3. Louisville Orchestra First Edition Records, Louisville, Kentucky (issued 1954 to the present).
4. Modern American Music, Columbia Records (later CBS, now SONY), New York, thirty-five discs.
5. Music in America/Society for the Preservation of the American Musical Heritage, New York (issued 1958–72); for complete list of fifty discs, see Hamm, p. 704.
6. New World Records/Recorded Anthology of American Music, New York (issued 1975 to the present); for partial list of more than two hundred discs, see Hamm, p. 695.
7. Nonesuch Records, New York; large catalog includes the most impressive American music repertoire of any commercial label.
8. Smithsonian Collection, Washington, D.C.; collections include classic jazz, classic country, American musical theater, and a comprehensive Duke Ellington series.

A word of caution: when listening to classical music, concentrate on complete works rather than skimming or browsing. Listen for the elusive clue to that organic quality from which we gain at one glance the total effect of a great building or a large painting. In music, as in literature, gaining that effect demands far more time and patience. Unfortunately there is no alternative: allow the time or miss the message.

Further Reading

Charles Hamm's *Music in the New World* (New York: Norton, 1983) is the most up-to-date, authoritative book on American music. It is referred to here as "Hamm." H. Wiley Hitchcock's *Music in the United States* (Englewood Cliffs: Prentice Hall, 1969, revised 1974) is a less exhaustive but perceptive treatment of the subject. Wilfred Mellers's *Music in a New Found Land* (New York: Oxford University Press, 1964) is a brilliant study of "themes and developments" (as its subtitle puts it) more than a thorough survey. It treats jazz with great respect but ignores rock. In earlier decades Gilbert Chase's *American Music* (New York: McGraw Hill, 1955, revised 1966) and John Tasker Howard's *Our American Music* (New York: Dodd, Mead, 1931, latest revision 1953) were widely read by laymen.

For a taste of how the most prominent composers viewed their craft and their society, see Aaron Copland's *The New Music* (New York: Norton, 1962); Charles Ives's *Essays before a Sonata* (New York: Norton, 1962); *Roger Sessions on Music* (Princeton: Princeton University Press, 1979) or John Cage's *Silence* (Middletown, Connecticut: Wesleyan University Press, 1961).

As a thorough study of popular song, Charles Hamm's *Yesterdays: Popular Song in America* (New York: Norton, 1979) is recommended, although devotees of the form should not miss Alec Wilder's *American Popular Song* (New York: Oxford University Press, 1972).

Among other special areas, jazz should be singled out for additional reading. Marshall Stearns's *The Story of Jazz* (New York: Macmillan, 1968) and Nat Hentoff's *The Jazz Life* (New York: Dial Press, 1961) are well worth investigating.

A final word about a unique chronicler of all the world's music, and America's especially—Nicholas Slonimsky. Reading the composer entries in his *Baker's Biographical Dictionary of Musicians* (New York: MacMillan, 8th ed., 1991) is a pleasure, and his *Music since 1900* (New York: Scribner's, 1971) both informs and entertains.

May what follows perform, in some degree, the same service for its readers.

Some Seeds Lie Dormant, Some Sprout

Most of us recognize the insistent rhythm of an American-Indian war dance. By the thousands American infants have been put to sleep or kept happy while awake by folksingers, part of whose repertoire has origins in the songs of the early English colonists. The Spanish settlers in the Southwest brought yet another distinctly different music to American shores. None of these first musical plantings took early root in the New World's fertile soil.

Perhaps Native-American chant was too primitive to interest the immigrant white man, but his equal ignorance of Indian language and philosophy left his descendants with considerable guilt about "Manifest Destiny." As for the folksongs from the Mother Country that musicologist Cecil Sharp (*English Folk Songs from the Southern Appalachians,* 1917) found alive and well in this century, they did not influence the classical music that Philadelphians, for example, heard around 1760 the way the Austrian *Ländler* (peasant dances in three-quarter time) affected so many of Haydn's symphonies.

Yet certain of these dormant strains were taken up in later centuries—naively by visiting celebrity Antonin Dvorak (Indian-style themes of the "New World" Symphony), more organically by first-generation American

---

Often overlooked in explaining the slow emergence of an American musical culture is the historic absence of arts patronage. Since the colonies were settled by opponents of noble and religious authority, a national policy against European-style aid to the arts was inevitable.

While the royal and papal "chapels" (professional performing ensembles) of the Renaissance supported their Josquins and Palestrinas, while Handel, Haydn and even Mozart were dependent on the eighteenth-century nobility, a deep American suspicion of such extravagance was taking root. It proved strong enough to last until the first appropriations to the National Endowment for the Arts in 1966.

Aaron Copland (who used the Shaker tune "Simple Gifts" in his ballet *Appalachian Spring*).

Gothic cathedrals, Renaissance painting, the music of Mozart and Beethoven—all came into being in cultures that had established a certain political stability and had experienced long cultural development. Throughout history, new nations have been too busy making roads and laws to concern themselves over much with cultivation of the arts. Music, like many other cultural resources, was often neglected as New World civilization unfolded.

Secular Art Music, Church Psalms, Music of the Slaves

Direct lines of descent can be traced, however, from other musical genes that were part of the New World pool during Revolutionary times. English and German hymns were the source of American church music, the country's first important sign of musical originality (see William Billings, p. 13). And those primitive drumbeats, those mournful outcries arriving from Africa by slave ship, were later transformed through plantation songs and funeral marches into twentieth-century jazz. But colonial Americans remained most firmly oriented to the art music of continental Europe, which was based on the do-re-mi scale and the straightforward major-minor harmonies that by the seventeenth century had replaced the more subtle Renaissance modal structures.

A few colonist sects like the Moravians even brought their instruments and scores with them. One curious example was the group of German Pietists led by Johannes Kelpius who debarked at Philadelphia around 1700 and took their fine violins, even a valuable organ, to live in a state of nature along the scenic Wissahickon Creek. Kelpius, his followers and their instruments were all wiped out within ten years. Their hymn tunes, among the few things to survive, would have sounded at home in the Rhineland.

The Moravians themselves, those idealistic and far more resourceful emigrants who called their new Pennsylvania home Bethlehem (founded 1741) were the first to make mainstream European music a part of ordinary life. Works of Mozart and Haydn appeared in their libraries not long after publication. Moreover, the Viennese-influenced chamber music of their first notable organist-composer, J. F. Peter, indicates that the scores did not sit unused on Bethlehem's shelves.

In nearby Philadelphia, a gentleman who signed his name Francis Hopkinson to both songs and the Declaration of Independence composed lines reminiscent of English airs:

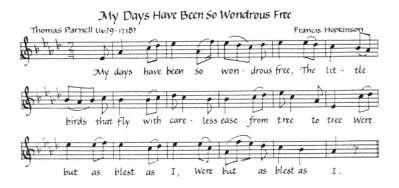

My Days Have Been So Wondrous Free

Thomas Parnell (1679-1718)   Francis Hopkinson

My days have been so won-drous free, The lit-tle birds that fly with care-less ease from tree to tree Were but as blest as I, Were but as blest as I.

Concert life in the colonial capital was active, thanks to the arrival from England in 1786 of composer Alexander Reinagle (1756–1809), who organized a series called City Concerts. His performance of Haydn overtures and Handel arias with a twenty-piece orchestra enabled Thomas Jefferson to satisfy his yearning for the music he missed at Monticello and may even have prompted Benjamin Franklin—who had to try everything once—to invent a new instrument, the glass harmonica.

Along with chamber music, more involved orchestra scores and even opera were heard. The "ballad opera" *Flora, or, Hob in the Wall* is the first piece of musical theater known to have been staged in the New World. It was produced in Charleston no later than 1735!

One area of colonial activity, hymn singing at church, acquired a crude but expressive musical style more suitable to worship in Boston than in London. Its emergence was due to the labors of America's first homegrown creative musician, William Billings (1746–1800). *The New England Psalm-Singer: or, American Chorister* (Boston, 1770), containing 126 original tunes by Billings, was the first truly worthy hymnbook in the colonies and was quickly recognized by the populace. One of the tunes, "Chester," supplied the music for the most popular patriotic song of the Revolution:

Chester (1770)

William Billings

Let ty-rants shake their i - ron rod, And slav'ry clank her gal - ling chains. We fear them not, -, we trust - in God. New England's God for - e - ver reigns

An eccentric, though ever more inspired, "singing school" teacher, Billings followed *The New England Psalm-Singer* with more discriminating and even better-received collections. But the "anthems, fuges and choruses" of his most advanced work, *The Psalm-Singer's Amusement* (1781), were aimed at more experienced choirs and revealed the composer's lack of polish more clearly.

Listening to Billings's rough-hewn version of English choral style (New World 205, 255 and 276) is an education in the intangible value of pure musical expression. Any attempt to

correct his "errors" would damage the touching sincerity of
the work's chordal movement and naive polyphony. Its over-
all effect, in the uplifting simplicity of the anthem "Jordan"
or the experimentally dissonant "Jargon," is beguiling.
William Billings was indeed an American composer with
"an ecstatic, visceral, almost transcendental sense of the
art" (Hamm, p. 149).

He was also, sadly, a musical pioneer in another respect.
Barely eking out a living from music and whatever other jobs
the considerate Bostonians found for him as street cleaner,
"sealer of leather," and pigpen tender, Billings was the first of
many American composers of note to die penniless. The year
was the first one of the new century.

Frontispiece for the *New England Psalm-Singer*
(William Billings, 1770), engraving by Paul Revere

Tentative Growth amid Imported Strains

Josef Skvorecky's *Dvorak in Love* (New York, 1986) is a novel about a great composer's attempt to locate the essential American musical spirit during three years spent in New York and Iowa (1892–95). Collecting Negro and Indian melodies, wandering city streets with his ears open to sounds of the people, Dvorak ended up producing a few masterworks no more "essential" to America (Symphony No. 8, "From the New World"; "American" Quartet, Op. 96) than Mendelssohn's *Scotch* Symphony is to Scotland or Bizet's *Carmen* to Spain.

History books on American music in the nineteenth century devote page after page to the influence of European immigrants from Reinagle to Dvorak, the German education of talented composers from George Whitefield Chadwick (1854–1931) to Edward MacDowell (1860–1908), and the strange symphonic products of Anthony Heinrich (1781–1861), who tried enshrining the western canyons musically one hundred years before Ferde Grofé's "Grand Canyon" Suite. (See the humorous description of Heinrich's "Grand" Symphony in *Dvorak in Love*, pp. 38–39.)

It makes a colorful story, but in the place of a native musical vigor one finds dutiful imitation and outright importation. Some derivative works of John Knowles Paine (1839–1906) are well worth hearing (for example, the Mass in D on New World 262/263). Horatio Parker (1863–1919) gave his students at Yale the solid academicism found in his music. Edward MacDowell, the most capable of later nineteenth-century figures, actually remained in Germany as a piano teacher for years after his student days there. Even MacDowell's more mature works— for example, *Twelve Virtuoso Studies*, Op. 46 (1894, recorded on New World 206), tend somehow to sound Mendelssohnian, Lisztian and Chopinesque by turns.

If there is an American strain in all this, it lies in a certain melodic sweetness found in the songs of Stephen Foster, the sentimental pieces of Ethelbert Nevin and MacDowell's immortal "To a Wild Rose." But far more strength lies in the piano compositions of a part-Creole virtuoso named Louis Moreau Gottschalk (1829–69), who was able at midcentury to make Caribbean melodies and rhythms into sophisticated music. Gottschalk's art is reminiscent of—but a world apart from—the paraphrases and transcriptions of Franz Liszt. Pieces like "The Banjo," "Souvenir de Porto Rico" and "La Gallina" (The Hen), far from historical curiosities, remain part of America's living musical heritage. Their syncopations and chromatic voice-leading can be simple but colorful touches:

Souvenir de Porto Rico, op. 31

(measure 68)   L. M. Gottschalk

Still, a Gottschalk or a MacDowell hardly constitutes a national school of composition, not for a nation that was already turning out its Emersons, Melvilles and Hawthornes. America's nineteenth century could hardly be called a time of great distinction where art music is concerned.

By contrast, American popular music did begin to sound "American" in the nineteenth century. Much of its native quality derived from the music of slaves both before and after emancipation. Minstrel shows, with their banjo-plunking caricatures of slaves conceived and performed by white people, were the first American entertainments to tour Europe (starting with a troupe called the Virginia Minstrels in 1844). After the Civil War, choirs at the newly established Negro colleges made what used to be spontaneous work songs of lamentation into the harmonized, respectable "spirituals" soon to be counted among the best American songs. Their familiar syncopations (later called "jazzy") and the shout-and-response device came from African roots, though such origins were much distorted by contact with white civilization.

Other worthy forms of popular music grew out of aspects of white society, notably American military bands and musical shows. Nineteenth-century milestones along the way to the modern band and Broadway theater—marches like

Songbook cover, Christy's Minstrels

D. W. Reeves's "Second Connecticut Regiment March" (1880) and shows like *The Black Crook* (1866)—may not enchant today's audiences, but they paved the way for world-recognized achievements belonging to the twentieth century.

In the realm of simple melody, secular and sacred, the nation expressed its inmost sentiments as it underwent westward expansion. Lowell Mason (1792–1872) built on the foundations laid by William Billings but ended by making the church music of Boston conform more closely to English models. More important, as the nation's first official municipal superintendent of public school music (Boston, 1838), he promulgated the idea that every American child should be taught to sing as well as to read. Paralleling that example, the spread of the great Civil War tunes ("Battle Hymn of the Republic," "Dixie," "Marching through Georgia") and the earliest cowboy songs showed the nation's desire to sing as much as to be sung to.

True, the impulse to sing is common wherever there is work to be done, and nineteenth-century America was only one of many places where the strength and virility of working people were expressed in song. But as will be seen, American popular music was to have its own brand of strength and virility.

Most writers on music consider 20th-century composing style diametrically opposed to the painting of pretty musical pictures, à la Edward MacDowell. Adolfo Salazar (in his landmark study, Music in Our Time, *New York, 1946, p. 310) makes a more subtle distinction. American music had progressed, he said, "from the agreeable picturesqueness of MacDowell to the aggressive picturesqueness of Aaron Copland."*

Salazar was writing in the early 1940s, as the word "aggressive" was acquiring a new and terrible meaning worldwide. His choice of words thus underlines, at the same time, the impact of modern innovation and the staying power—musically speaking—of 19th-century sentiment, concord, romance.

A Rugged Genius and a Profusion of Pop

Classical Music: Finding a New Voice

Henry Adams, proud New Englander who foresaw a spiritual awakening in twentieth-century America after the technological miracle of the nineteenth, would have been happy to know that the first steps toward an indigenous style of composition were taken by the son of a Connecticut bandmaster just after the century began.

His name was Charles Ives (1874–1954), and the reason Adams didn't know of him is that the music world itself didn't. Ives had studied under Horatio Parker at Yale (1894–98), then earned a fortune in the insurance business while composing after work with little thought of public performance.

Whether from the resultant stress or a notably restive nature, he suffered a severe heart attack and stroke in midlife that ended any possibility of his promoting his work or influencing other composers. Compare, for example, Frank Lloyd Wright's influence on architecture or the spread of Arts and Crafts design ideas contemporary with Ives. It remained for the next generation to discover the music and be influenced by it. "His music was not so much ignored as it was totally unknown. . . . Had he persevered . . . in the first two decades of the century, a viable school of American composition might have become a reality" (Hamm, pp. 436–7).

Ives's most advanced work, the Symphony No. 4 (1910–16), conveys an impression of great, almost cavernous

Mr. and Mrs. Charles Ives, during the composer's long retirement

space filled with chaotic motion (the second movement's cacophony) combined with serenity (the slow fugue of the third movement). As a prelude, Ives sets a choral hymn by Lowell Mason ("Watchman, tell us of the night") against string masses and brass punctuation that suggest starting the day, and in the finale a dirge gives way to a slow processional.

Those who know the contemporaneous symphonies of Mahler see a marked contrast between the monumental European and the rugged American, whose ruggedness is especially apparent in his dissonant sound. It is an intensely organized sound, giving off, through fragmented familiar melodies ("In the Sweet Bye and Bye," "Turkey in the Straw") and thickly augmented harmonies, a deceptive sense of looseness or even improvisation. Repeated listening leads one to expect the unexpected as well as to respect the tightness of the structure. The same can be said of the landmark "Concord" Piano Sonata (1919), where the main motive echoes Beethoven's Fifth Symphony, and of the deceptively rambling song, "General William Booth Enters into Heaven" (1914).

In the music of Charles Ives, William Billings's American individualism reappears after a century's dutiful obeisance to European tradition. The paradox is that Billings, the simple choirmaster, worked in public view; Ives, the prosperous businessman, labored largely in obscurity.

Musical obscurity was epidemic in Ives's day. Among his most important contemporaries, only Charles Griffes (1884–1920) and Carl Ruggles (1876–1971) made a real effort to find musical expression for the dawning American century. Both were little recognized while alive.

After composing in a French manner, with more of Debussy's mistiness than Ravel's clarity, Griffes wrote a Piano Sonata (1918, New World 273) showing much of the same sprawling cragginess that Ives put into his "Concord" Sonata. He taught at a private school near New York City, tried desperately to find a public there and died young.

Ruggles also wrote craggy orchestral works with titles like *Angels* (1920), *Portals* (1926) and *Sun Treader* (1926). Though he lived into old age, through disillusionment he withdrew from active composing life without making any strong impact. Today his music is respected, recorded and analyzed for traces of first-growth Americanism.

For the rest of the concert world just before and after 1900, a continuing deference to Europe, and particularly Germany, was the norm. MacDowell's *Woodland Sketches* (1896) and the opera *Natoma* (1911) by Victor Herbert (1859–1924) used Native-American themes but conventional harmonies that took the art no farther westward than Dvorak's "New World" Symphony.

As the 1920s began, the nation still awaited an indigenous composer with enough originality and free spirit to rally a truly American school.

Popular Music: Reflecting New World Optimism

Victor Herbert's name brings up the central event in American music at the turn of the century, namely, the sudden spread of its popular or entertainment forms throughout the world. Herbert's operettas *Babes in Toyland* (1903) and *Naughty Marietta* (1910) were a part of this development. His classical background (concert cellist, member of the Metropolitan Opera orchestra by 1896) suggests that his heart was really in the not-very-successful operas he wrote later, but Herbert's operetta melodies had the immediate appeal of popular song.

So did the marches of John Philip Sousa (1854–1932). The "Stars and Stripes Forever" (1896) and "Semper Fidelis" (1895) made Sousa's Marine Band as familiar in amusement parks and concert halls as dance bands would later be in college gymnasiums.

But the American dance band is related to marching in another way. Out of processional marches and the minstrel show "Cakewalks" came the not altogether respectable style called ragtime. Its most gifted composer, Scott Joplin (1868–1917), persevered in emphasizing ragtime's lyric rather than its earthy character, as, for example in the wistful waltz "Bethena":

Bethena – A Concert Waltz
(1905)
Scott Joplin

Joplin's talent, most advanced in the full-length opera *Treemonisha* (1911), had to wait for a ragtime revival more than fifty years after his death to be fully appreciated.

The story of how jazz began in the black marching bands at New Orleans funerals and took over the downtown bawdy houses, then the night life of Memphis and St. Louis, before flowering in Chicago during the twenties has been well told (for example in Marshall Stearns's *The Story of Jazz,* New York, 1956). A good place to hear it with matchless color is the Library of Congress's recorded testimony (*The Saga of Mr. Jelly Lord*, 12 albums, issued by Riverside Records RLP 9001-12, New York, 1938) by Ferdinand "Jelly Roll" Morton (1885–1941), whose Red Hot Peppers made some of the first records of original jazz (Chicago, 1926). All five players (trumpet, trombone, clarinet, drums and piano) were black. They played without music; many would not

The Scott Joplin postage stamp, issued 1982

have been able to read musical scores even if jazz had been a written instead of an improvised style.

Louis Armstrong (1900–1971) is the New Orleans native whose unique career spanned this early development of jazz and its later glamorization through television.

Perhaps the summit of jazz accomplishment after 1929 lay in the sophisticated songs ("Mood Indigo" in 1930, "Do Nothing 'til You Hear from Me" in 1943) and concert works (for example, the hour-long *Black, Brown and Beige* in 1943) of Edward "Duke" Ellington (1899–1974). But from their first Cotton Club date in 1927 to their later world tours, the Ellington band (already twelve strong by the late twenties) preserved the best brassiness of jazz while giving it a new suavity.

While jazz was taking its course up the Mississippi, another popular-music shift was in progress farther east. Song publishers in Boston, Philadelphia and other cities were giving way to New York's Tin Pan Alley (so-called from the "tinny" sound of upright pianos hawking the new songs).

Like the Irish-American Victor Herbert and the Portuguese-American John Philip Sousa, many Tin Pan Alley composers

---

Jazz and its origins in the American South have fascinated Europeans throughout the 1900s, even in the fifties, when jazz musicians could barely find enough audiences inside the United States to provide a living.

Black musicians from "Duke" to "Dizzy" were being greeted by large crowds in Stockholm and Paris when Woodstock was drawing the first throngs for rock (1969). Saxophonist Dexter Gordon (1923–90, later star of the film Round Midnight*), drummer Sydney Bechet (1891–1959) and others made their homes abroad. Meanwhile visitors from France and Sweden (not to mention Germany and Japan) often included New Orleans in their sightseeing itineraries, searching for the authentic flavor of jazz.*

One American jazz buff, listening to German radio soon after World War II, was amused to hear a recording of "Black Bottom" introduced as performed by Marmaladenkuchen ("Jelly Roll") Morton.

came from families outside mainstream America—notably Irving Berlin (1888–1989) and George Gershwin (1899–1937), from Russian-Jewish stock, and another Irish-American named George M. Cohan (1878–1942). What secret ingredient lent their music, as well as that of black musicians from North and South, the global appeal no other world culture could match during the unfolding century?

To answer the question, we need only select a few pieces from the surface of memory, where they are stored right next to "Stars and Stripes"—Cohan's "Yankee Doodle Boy" (1904), Berlin's "Alexander's Ragtime Band" (1911), Gershwin's "Swanee" (1919). A certain optimism, candor and energy sets them apart from the Viennese operetta tunes, French love songs and German cabaret music that competed with them for the ears of the world.

That very quality pervades the first musical comedy masterpiece to evolve from the new popular wave, *Show Boat* (1927) by Jerome Kern (1885–1945). Less popular than Paul Robeson made "Ol' Man River" or Helen Morgan made "Bill" in the same show, the song "Make Believe" might offer a good case in point:

Make Believe (1927)

Jerome Kern

Kern achieves a happy flow in this fine song by contrasting the long-short-long-short-long motive with walking long notes, leaps with scalewise motion and a pervading regularity with little surprises like the triplet in measure 6 and the sharp in measure 26. Putting chords beneath the melody is a beginner's joy; of the standard thirty-two bars, only measures 23 to 27 offer any resistance.

Popular music critic Alec Wilder was right to call "Make Believe" "the kind of song so strong and of a piece that its harmonic nature is of no consequence" (*American Popular Song*, p. 58). In its simplicity, its wholesome C-major purity, the song reflects the well-being of an uncrowded, uncomplicated society just two years before the stock market crash was to complicate matters considerably.

If simplicity and optimism predominated in early twentieth-century popular music, America's troubles were still perceptible. Jazz may have been born as a kind of celebration of freedom, but the blues went along side by side with it, lamenting the past. Ragtime also shows its darker color when played at moderate speed, as intended.

A similar relationship existed between Tin Pan Alley and the Old World longing and sadness of Yiddish musicals, which flourished for a time (1880–1940) in New York. Hamm is doubtless right in suggesting that Jewish songwriters, in their urge to assimilate, deliberately kept Yiddish darkness out of their work. It was not Berlin, Gershwin, Kern or Richard Rodgers (1902–79) but a non-Jewish member of the song-writing pantheon, Cole Porter (1892–1964), who admitted it. Not only in the obvious Yiddish flavor of "My Heart Belongs to Daddy" (1939) but also in minor-mode songs like "Why Should I Care" (1937) and "Silk Stockings" (1954) (see examples), Porter intentionally used this underestimated resource. But that was later, after he had shared musically in the unique, world-uplifting optimism of pre-1929 America.

Why Should I Care?

Cole Porter

Why should I care when my sweetheart is there?

Why should I cry if the tax-es go sky high?

Silk Stockings

Cole Porter

Silk stockings, I touch them and find the

joys that re-mind me of you

Avant-Garde Music: Shocking the Bourgeoisie

Another development in American music of the early twentieth century was the appearance of compositions intended to unsettle, to disturb, often to shock—in other words, music of an *avant-garde*.

Not only the term (borrowed from the military) but the idea itself originated in France. A talented Parisian named Edgard Varèse (1883–1965) began composing and conducting before World War I, emigrated to America in 1915, and conceived the style he later described as "bodies of intelligent sounds moving freely in space." We can get an idea of how consistently Varèse pursued this concept by comparing his sixteen-minute *Arcana* (1927) for large orchestra (including eight percussionists playing forty different instruments) with the later, twenty-five-minute *Deserts* (1954) for winds and percussion.

As much as any thinking musician in Paris, Varèse was influenced by the furor over Stravinsky's *Rite of Spring* (1913), with its primitive beats and wails sounding deceptively avant-garde to many. *Arcana*'s bursts of drum-punctuated sound are no more disturbing than *Rite of Spring*, but the shafts of sudden solo instrumental sunlight and the free percussion wanderings point in the direction of the title—that is, toward mystery, in this case, the mysteries of space.

Where *Arcana* is built from sound masses, *Deserts* seems constructed out of points of chance collision among weightless sounds (compare with pointillism, the use of small dabs of paint to create an illusion of solidity). The effect is far freer, with the wandering element now changed into the lugubrious air of a slow-fading foghorn or a duet between xylophone and kettledrums. If *Arcana* ends in a certain cloud of mystery, *Deserts* whistles off wildly, disturbingly, into outer space. Both pieces test our ability to perceive musical form. One clue is Varèse's reference to *Deserts* as music of "crystallized sound" with the "limitless external forms" of crystal.

Avant-garde music is hard enough for musicians to penetrate. One suggestion for the uninitiated is to avoid the tendency to take it only in short doses. Varèse's ability to make an important point while administering his obligatory shock requires hearing him through a complete work.

In America, Varèse had considerable influence on native-born, avant-garde composers:

1. Henry Cowell (1897–1965) shocked his public in *Aeolian Harp* (1923) with what he called "tone clusters" (keyboard dissonances made with closed fist).
2. Harry Partch (1901–76) invented a whole family of instruments incorporating "microtones" (made by dividing the octave into more than the conventional twelve "semitones"). With his instruments he fashioned large-scale stage works well worth reviving (for example,

Revelation in the Courthouse Park, based on Euripides'
Bacchae, which reaches levels of dance-accompanied
frenzy beyond the range of normal instruments).
3. John Cage (b. 1912), Cowell's student, is discussed in the
   next chapter.

A group of microtonal instruments designed by Harry Partch

Jolting the cultural world into awareness of new ideas became the function of this new phenomenon in music, as it was
of Dada and surrealism in the other arts. But it was one thing
for such developments to originate in Paris, France. That the
United States of America could have its own musical avant-
garde was a sure sign of its coming-of-age.

The Twentieth-Century Concert Audience: Losing the Connection

One of the most difficult challenges to writers on the arts in
Western civilization is explaining the gap that opened
between artists and laymen around 1900.

In music, the late compositions of Mozart and Beethoven—suddenly more complex in mood and structure than the main body of their work—seem to provide a precedent. Fans of the film *Amadeus* will recall the scene in which Mozart hears his emperor's opinion that *The Marriage of Figaro* has "too many notes." But Mozart's prolixity and Beethoven's flights of imagination in the final quartets and sonatas did not lead their Austro-German successors—Weber, Mendelssohn, Wagner, Brahms—toward the same estrangement from the listening public, which in fact flocked to hear the later composers.

It remained for France to harbor, in the music of Hector Berlioz (1803–69) and most significantly Claude Debussy (1862–1918), those tendencies toward freedom in building musical materials and shaping forms that eventually outdistanced most of the audience. One clue to this music lies in its dimensions; Berlioz's *Requiem* (1837), with its monster forces (huge chorus, inflated brass, eight kettledrums), became the prototype not only for oversized works to come (Wagner's *Ring*, Mahler's Symphony No. 8) but for the very idea of expecting from the average listener a new preoccupation with detail.

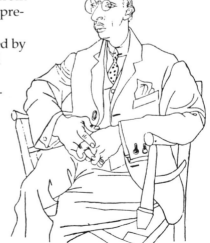

Debussy was not attracted by the vogue for long-winded composition, though we need only think of his best-known piece, *Prelude to the Afternoon of a Fawn*, (1892), to feel how enigmatic his voice can sound next to those of his contemporaries: Gustav Mahler (1860–1911), Edward Elgar

Picasso's drawing of Stravinsky

(1857–1934) and Giacomo Puccini (1858–1924). A large-scale Debussy work such as *La Mer* (*The Sea*, 1905) casts the first-time listener somewhat adrift, its waves of fragmented melody in motion over chords piled high for richness. With his tone-painting magic, Debussy ultimately finds safe harbor. *La Mer* has become an orchestral standard, but the composer's only opera, *Pelléas et Mélisande* (1902), is the first of many twentieth-century masterpieces that are too introspective and difficult to please the general public.

This indifference to the public, which was a reaction to nineteenth-century romanticism, had its most far-reaching effect in Vienna. Arnold Schoenberg (1874–1951), a brilliant composer of acceptably tonal music (for example, the string sextet, *Transfigured Night*, 1899), suddenly presented to the world a set of short piano pieces (Opus 11, 1909) in which all semblance of a tonal center was avoided. Atonality was born; music had found freedom, not only from the past, but from the need to please the majority.

Not every turn-of-the-century composer displeased his audience. Maurice Ravel (1875–1937), for example, was able to give pleasure and a degree of challenge through judicious use of dissonance, exoticism, rhythmic innovation. But most masters of the time—Stravinsky, Bartok, Hindemith, Prokofiev—felt the pressure to seek and find some new answer to the creative problem that simmered through the nineteenth century and erupted like a volcano in the music of Schoenberg.

Classical Species and Rampant Rock

Four Classical Categories

If the Great War of 1914–18 effectively killed the notion of a carefree, ocean-insulated America, the Great Depression and World War II were its public requiem. With World War I an old order did indeed disappear. Afterwards, all manner of things American began assuming organized shape, as though in hasty preparation for world leadership.

According to that trend, American concert music after 1929 can be said to be divisible into four principal groupings, which in this study are named for their first and most prominent representatives (see the table, p. 34–35). By 1939 each had a generating European force behind it (the "preceptors" with asterisks) and the potential to emerge dominant over the other groupings.

First to show that potential was the Copland group. Its namesake, who was in Paris by 1921, ready for the influence of the celebrated French teacher, Nadia Boulanger, was New York's Aaron Copland (1900–90). Starting in the thirties, Copland's style of composing attained international status for American music.

But by the end of the 1950s German expressionism, which gave a quite different density to the music of Brooklyn-born Roger Sessions (1896–1985) and Boston's Elliott Carter (b. 1908), had come to seem the only true and valid path.

While this competition among metropolitan composers was beginning, a "micropolitan" from Oklahoma, Roy Harris (1898–1979), was combining elements of French and German traditions with a certain harmonic austerity to make American music in a new mold. This style, too, had a brief ascendancy before and after World War II.

So did the neoromantic works of Samuel Barber (1910–81) and neo-Puccinian operas of Gian Carlo Menotti (b. 1911), products of the composers' studies at Philadelphia's new and conservative Curtis Institute of Music (founded 1924). Romanticism, perhaps not so "neo," also infused the writing of Howard Hanson (1896–1981), who for forty years (1924–64) directed Rochester's Eastman School of Music.

Though they turned dormant during the fifties and sixties, neither the Harris nor the Barber group ever conceded victory to the first two. Public resistance to Sessions group style remained suppressed during these decades, but the group's use of dissonance, its angular melodies, above all its harmonic complexity, gained no stronger audience allegiance than Schoenberg himself had earned earlier in Vienna.

The virtual flood of new American composition during this period fits, with an occasional tight squeeze, into these four slots, defined by certain basic style characteristics which we must now examine more closely. Aaron Copland's music has a durability and significance for the larger public that are remarkable among his contemporaries. If we listen to a concert work like the jazzy Piano Concerto (1926), a pictorial orchestral piece like *El Salon Mexico* (1936), the film score for *Our Town* (1940) or one of the ballets, say *Rodeo* (1942), we immediately hear the composer's drive, vigor and conciseness, as opposed to any tendency to be cerebral, frivolous or long-winded. This is the aspect of Copland known to most music-loving Americans who normally do not seek out twentieth-century repertoire. It can be deeply moving indeed to first-time listeners, as in the main theme of *A Lincoln Portrait* (1942):

NAME	DERIVES FROM
Copland Group	French Post-Impressionism and Neo-Classicism
Sessions Group	German Post-Romanticism and Expressionism
Harris Group	Central European Nationalism
Barber Group	Italian/Russian/Nordic Romanticism

CHARACTERISTICS	PRECEPTORS
• Tonal but piquant harmony • Emphasis on monophony • Conciseness • Basic mood: serenity • Contrasting with: wit, ardor	*Stravinsky

• Chromatic harmony and melody,
   whether atonal or not
• Emphasis on polyphony
• Expansiveness
• Basic mood: agitation
• Contrasting with: ironic
   humor, fervor
	*Schoenberg
	*Hindemith

• Tonal but austere harmony
• Equal emphasis on monophony and
   polyphony
• Breadth of line, tempered by folk-
   flavor
• Basic mood: earnestness
• Contrasting with: joy, pride
	*Bartok

• Tonality unabashed • Emphasis on lyricism • Basic mood: self-concern • Contrasting with: gaiety, emotional expression	Puccini, *Rachmaninoff, Sibelius

*U.S. Residents by 1939

Another, more esoteric aspect can be heard in such chamber compositions as the Piano Variations (1930), Piano Fantasy (1957) and Flute/Piano Duo (1971). Here Copland turns introspective, writes motives instead of extended melodies and uses more abrasive sonorities. His *Connotations,* (1969), written for the opening of New York's Lincoln Center, followed twelve-tone procedures throughout.

Piano Fantasy (1955-7)

Aaron Copland

Aaron Copland and Robert Palmer, 1941

By reaching two publics and by articulating his intentions clearly, Copland exerted strong influence during much of the century, attaining the unofficial title "dean of American composers."

Roger Sessions started in a similar direction with *Black Maskers* (1923), a suite of incidental music showing a darker strain than Copland's—tonal but dissonant, tightly scored and dramatically expressive. In cosponsoring New York's Copland-Sessions concerts later in the twenties, he also seemed to seek an influential role as Americans grew more responsive to their native culture. But the nine symphonies and many other concertos, chamber works and operas that followed

Symbolizing the paradox of a competition in American music between two main schools—French and Germanic—World War II happened to cast its most famous musical refugees up on the same American shore. During the 1940s, Igor Stravinsky and Arnold Schoenberg both made Los Angeles their home for the remainder of their lives.

It was paradoxical because the two European tendencies—to be sardonically good-humored (French) and to be soberly pensive (German)—always existed side by side in the American mind. Stravinsky had long fascinated young Americans across the Atlantic with the accentuated meters (irregular but classic in spirit) and pungent harmonies (dissonant but tone-centered) he used to fashion "neoclassicism." Schoenberg's "Composition in Twelve Tones," appearing to reject the past by giving all twelve semitones in the octave equal importance, attracted different disciples.

But Stravinsky himself, after Schoenberg's death (1951) and the subsequent elevation of atonality and dodecaphonism to predominant status, began experimenting with expressionist methods in his ballet Agon *(1957). George Balanchine, who choreographed it, later used the music of Schoenberg's disciple Anton Webern (1883–1945) for his landmark work,* Episodes *(1959). Even Aaron Copland tried twelve-tone writing (see p. 36). French and German streams began to flow into one musical Mississippi. The distance between them began to shrink. Like the two aging refugees in southern California, French and German modernism had been American neighbors all along.*

leaned more and more—in effect if not dogma—toward the atonal style of Schoenberg with its stark melodic and worried harmonic character.

So did Elliott Carter's complex sonatas and string quartets (No. 1 in 1951, No. 2 in 1959). Introducing a new concept by assigning different sets of tempo changes to each of the four instruments, these works are fiendishly difficult for both performer and listener. Carter wrote that he intended his new way of composing to "present, as human experience often does, certain emotionally charged events . . . producing often a kind of irony, which I am particularly interested in." Despite his desire to make contact with the public, none of Carter's prolific output, not even his organic Variations for Orchestra (1955) or the ingenious Double Concerto for Harpsichord, Piano and Orchestra (1961), won the repeated performances demanded of Copland's ballets. What they did win is praise from critics, other musicians and a small but vocal audience of connoisseurs—especially those attuned to Austro-German expressionist art.

Roy Harris's Third Symphony (1937) introduced an element that neither Copland nor the expressionist-oriented wing had sought—the spiritual simplicity and breadth of the American landscape, independent of identifiable folk ingredients. Austere, "open" harmonies (that is, tending to omit the rich center note, or "third" tone, of the triad) and full, sweeping melody lines carried his message, somewhat the way Bartok's music built on its Hungarian folk basis. Copland's style, often linked with that of Harris, had some of the fullness but not the sweep one almost feels from seeing a page of the score of the Harris symphony.

One of the paradoxes in this exciting period is that the great success of the Third Symphony at its 1939 premiere by the Boston Symphony Orchestra was never repeated in Harris's long and productive lifetime. At age seventy-eight, in 1976, he had the satisfaction of seeing the Philadelphia Orchestra

Symphony No. 3

Roy Harris

take the Third Symphony to China, though that choice at that historic moment may have pointed more to safe, non-troublesome content than to any lasting influence the piece exerted.

Barber, Menotti and, in lesser degree, Hanson managed to continue using nineteenth-century practices while avoiding in various ways the derivative stamp of Paine, Parker and MacDowell half a century before them (see p. 16): Barber by the subtle contouring of melody and arrangement of texture in his deeply affecting song cycles (for example, *Knoxville: Summer of 1915*, written in 1947), Menotti by deft orchestration and cogent sonorities in his operas (especially *The Medium*

in 1946, *The Consul* in 1950), and Hanson by the Sibelius-influenced power of his operatic/symphonic concepts (notably in the "Romantic" Symphony of 1930 and the opera *Merry Mount* of 1933).

Such were the main musical currents of this time and their main exponents. Was any one of them more entitled to leadership of the emerging "American School" than "Dean" Aaron Copland? Before deciding that, we need to look more closely at the ever-growing ranks beneath these key names.

A quick count of recognized American composers reaching maturity in the years 1929–68 produces a total well above one hundred. Names like Norman Dello Joio, Morton Gould and Vincent Persichetti appear on concert programs with some frequency; others, like Arthur Berger, Irving Fine, Leon Kirchner, Otto Luening and Milton Babbitt do not (nor do scores of the generation that followed, trained by this first group at that uniquely American musical oasis, the university). This is not the place to offer complete lists of such composers, or to accord due credit for accomplishments, but only to note the clues to what's happening in American music.

Selecting six names at random for closer inspection, we arrive at a list that includes both the celebrated and the lesser known: Robert Palmer (b. 1915), Leonard Bernstein (1918–90), George Rochberg (b. 1918), Leslie Bassett (b. 1923), Gunther Schuller (b. 1925) and Samuel Adler (b. 1928). Where do these six fall in the four-group "classification of species"?

Samuel Barber and Gian Carlo Menotti

Robert Palmer's productive but frustrating career says volumes about this chapter in American music. Very much a disciple of Roy Harris but with a characteristically sober tinge to his writing, he was singled out by Aaron Copland in a 1947 *New York Times* article as "one of the four most promising" young U.S. composers. Reinforcing that view, the Koussevitzky Foundation commissioned his Piano Quartet (1945), which was recorded by Columbia (M-4842) and later published in a prestigious Peters edition. It bore the Harris stamp in its harmonic austerity, Bela Bartok's influence in its rhythms and the composer's own wistful sense of melody.

Palmer, the disciple of indigenous nationalism, remained faithful to Harris group principles in the writing of four string quartets, three piano sonatas and numerous other extended chamber works during a long career at Cornell University. As the trend towards dodecaphonic music took hold in the 1950s, Palmer dropped from sight and composed few large-scale orchestral works. If more existed, they would probably have been passed over by the Boston Symphony or the Los Angeles—not to mention the New York—Philharmonic anyway.

An example of what the music public missed thereby is contained in the Concerto for Piano, String Orchestra and Timpani (1969)—three solidly constructed movements of classic proportions—and in the Third Piano Sonata (1979) with its slow-movement fugue theme seeming to grow organically from the preceding stately dance (see example, next page).

Leonard Bernstein was certainly the most likely heir, considering his rare ability to communicate in early works like the ballet *Fancy Free* (1944) and *The Age of Anxiety* (Symphony No. 2, 1949), to the mantle of Copland. But unlike his idol Gustav Mahler, he proved unable to pursue one of the century's most brilliant conducting careers and remain productive as composer. There are signs in the later works—*Mass* (opening at Washington's Kennedy Center in 1971) and *Divertimento* (composed for the Boston Symphony's centenary in 1980)—of consistency at the expense of inspiration, adding up to a different kind of frustration from Robert Palmer's. Even Leonard Bernstein the conductor, with all his influence and fame, could not program enough Copland group music to surmount the expressionist tide after midcentury.

George Rochberg, after serving in World War II, started composing in a conservative (Barber group) style under the influence of Rosario Scalero and Gian Carlo Menotti at Curtis Institute. What happened in the 1950s can be heard by listening to the profound but tonal Symphony No. 1 (1949) and then to the atonal Twelve Bagatelles (1952) with its jagged piano lines reflecting the world of Schoenberg. Rochberg had been transformed into a definitive atonalist and was soon turning out younger exponents of atonality at the University of Pennsylvania.

But this was only the first of his transformations on the way to becoming one of the nation's most respected Sessions group composers. Just three years before the end of the period under discussion, in 1965, he wrote *Music for the Magic Theater*. Reacting to the world of Hermann Hesse's *Steppenwolf*, Rochberg opened and closed in his expressionist style but

Third Piano Sonata
(Canzona - Fuga - Canzona)

Robert Palmer

composed an entire middle movement in the spirit of Mozart. This procedure would later be known as "collage," a term borrowed from painting.

Leslie Bassett is a Californian whose natural attraction to expressionist procedures never modified a certain brightness and curving looseness in his musical lines. The sonorous punctuation he employs is richly burnished, however, and the scores he constructed carefully during a long University of Michigan teaching career did much to gain respect for expressionist ideas in the Midwest. *Music for Saxophone and Piano* (1968, recorded on New World 209)—with a freely notated finale that uses no set meter—is a good example of his mature style. Bassett is an exemplary member of the Sessions group.

Less exemplary but more notable as an expressionist disciple is Gunther Schuller, French horn player and self-taught composer who rose to the top of his profession (president of the New England Conservatory, director of the Berkshire Music Center at Tanglewood) by way of jazz performance.

Does Art take its cue from life, or vice versa? What happened to American concert music after 1950 argues strongly for the latter. While life during the Eisenhower presidency was, despite McCarthyism and the hydrogen bomb, comparatively secure and prosperous, America's serious music foretold unrest. To be sure, few were listening. The almanac for four separate years tells the story:

1951: *Stravinsky shows his stylistic self-assurance by presenting—at age sixty-nine—his first and only full-length opera,* The Rake's Progress. *Leonard Bernstein leads the belated first performance of Ives's Symphony No. 2 (completed 1902) at the New York Philharmonic. Menotti introduces* Amahl and the Night Visitors, *and Martha Graham makes a ballet about Saint Joan to tonal music of Norman Dello Joio. Expressionism remains an alternative way of composing. Schoenberg dies, age seventy-six, somewhat disappointed with the fate of his "dodecaphonism." Aaron Copland's Piano Quartet, however, foretells a different future: for the first time the Copland group's title composer tries the Sessions group's twelve-tone approach to music.*

Inventing the term "third stream" to describe concert music incorporating jazz, he ultimately found the Sessions group style most compatible with—or perhaps most apt to meet a certain need for seriousness in—the inherent freedom of jazz.

Schuller's *Seven Studies on Themes of Paul Klee* (1959, recorded on Mercury MG-50282) is a tonal composition with a jazz picture of the painter's impish *Kleiner Blauteufel* ("Little Blue Devil") followed by a serially constructed impression of *Die Zwitschermachine* ("Twittering Machine"). The popularity of *Seven Studies* spread Schuller's reputation as an expressionist who is accessible to ordinary listeners. That impression is reinforced by a prolific output, including concertos for many instruments, symphonic works and an opera, *The Visitation* (1966), based on Kafka's *The Trial*.

Samuel Adler, a composer who often emphasized Jewish musical sources, fits rather tightly into the nationalist (Harris) group. His father was cantor at the synagogue in Mannheim, Germany, but found refuge from Hitler in the United States

1957: *Roger Sessions's serially organized Symphony No. 3 and Stravinsky's expressionist-influenced* Agon *are the major new works. Bernstein, elevated to the directorship of the New York Philharmonic, finds himself hard pressed to locate new tonal scores of value, though he prefers tonality over atonality; as a composer he experiences writing block in varying degrees.*

1960: *Premieres like Pierre Boulez's atonal* Pli selon pli *("Fold according to Fold") in Europe and George Rochberg's serial* Time-Span *at Home reflect the playing out of a remarkable displacement, which was later confirmed by the appointment of Boulez to replace Bernstein in New York (1970).*

1968: *The nation hears its president decline reelection. Daily life thus follows in the direction expressionism has been pointing—toward stress, tension and psychological unraveling. Hardly a responsible young composer emerges who writes tonal music. The triumph of dodecaphonism is, for the time being, complete, though signs of a countermovement have already appeared (see Rochberg, p. 52).*

when Samuel was eleven years old. Adler often uses Jewish musical sources, without being preoccupied with them. Though atonal techniques are not strange to him, he employs them only for special needs while composing mainly in a tonal, contrapuntal style. By the eighties, celebrating synagogue occasions with a commission to this distinguished Eastman School professor became common practice, but Adler is also known as a symphonist and as an opera and chamber music composer. The nervous movement and spare sonorities of his Trio (1964) contrast with the freer, less tonal sound of his *Aeolus, God of the Winds* (1978) for clarinet, violin, cello and piano. Both works (recorded on Gasparo GS-252C) show the sturdy, architectural sense of Harris group composers, but *Aeolus* leans in the Sessions group direction.

Each of these gifted, well-prepared Americans—as well as many like them—found the four principal composing categories a part of his environment as he came to maturity in the thirties and forties. These composers did not have to grope in isolation, as Charles Ives had to, for an American idiom but could slip into (or out of) a particular group, according to their individual makeup.

But they did have to face another of Ives's problems—the indifference or hostility of a public unaccustomed to innovation. Uncompromising dissonance, strange ways of building forms and melodies, and experiments with harmonies never captivated the large public gained, for example, by Gershwin's Piano Concerto in F or *American in Paris*. None of the "second generation" of twentieth-century composers ever acquired an adequate audience in the concert hall (though Menotti and Bernstein did so on Broadway).

Before the seventies, only Aaron Copland was able to speak repeatedly in a sophisticated syntax to large numbers of listeners. Perhaps that's what entitles him to his honorary deanship.

The Burgeoning Popular Music Field

Out of the great surge of popular song, jazz and ragtime before and just after World War I came decades of expansion in every segment of American entertainment music—the big bands named Miller, Dorsey and Herman (playing Tin Pan Alley songs far more than jazz), the less celebrated but no less important black bands like Jimmy Lunceford's, the Hollywood films with their symphonic-size orchestras and the Broadway shows (Richard Rodgers's *Oklahoma* in 1943, Frank Loesser's *Guys and Dolls* in 1950, Frederick Loewe's *My Fair Lady* in 1956) that were so far ahead of *Showboat* in pace and integration (if not in musical invention).

Jan Clayton and John Raitt in *Carousel*, 1945

Rodgers and Hammerstein's *Carousel* (1945) is generally seen as a landmark in the interweaving of dance and dramatic solo (Billy Bigelow's "Soliloquy") into the American musical, though Gershwin's *Porgy and Bess* had already accomplished that feat in 1935. Both shows were later to be considered worthy of performance in opera houses.

But as momentous as the first half of the years 1929–68 were, as synonymous as Benny Goodman's swing clarinet, Louis Armstrong's jazz trumpet and Duke Ellington's suave harmonies became with up-to-date living and loving world-wide, the fifties and sixties surpassed them. First to augur major changes (around 1945) was the bewildering "bebop" music of Charlie Parker and Dizzy Gillespie. As baroque musicians had done two centuries earlier, they made melodic embellishment into a kind of preoccupation and opened the way for innovations that soon multiplied. Gillespie tried to keep the new style intelligible; Parker stubbornly emphasized its complexity. William Austin, the first musicologist to accord jazz its proper role in music history, considers Parker's music to require "for discriminating appreciation as thorough a specialized preparation as any 'classical' style" (*Music in the Twentieth Century*, New York, 1966, p. 291).

Country music, growing out of the simple squareness of folksong, had its own rural audience in the first half of the century and its own instrument—the guitar. Before World War II an American could grow up in a small city without ever hearing the country guitar-playing on the farms just outside of town, or on the first rural radio stations.

Bluegrass music, adding its exhilarating banjo-fiddle sound around the mid-forties, was the first related development to attract the attention of urban—usually sophisticated rather than working class—listeners.

By 1960 the sons of city people were leaving home to learn country styles in "the sticks." Roy Acuff (star of Nashville's

"Grand Ole Opry" in the forties) and Gene Autry were no longer exotic figures; city dwellers swarmed to "folk-style" guitar classes, and guitar sales boomed.

It was the "gentrification" of white country music, combined with offshoots of black jazz called boogie-woogie and rhythm and blues (R & B) that led the way around 1955 into "rock 'n roll"—or more simply "rock"—a kind of insistent-beat music with the same simple chord basis as country western but far heavier accents and far less genteel love lyrics than country ever had. Since it came out of cities like Cincinnati ("Good Rockin' Tonight," 1947, by Wynonie Harris) and Philadelphia ("Rock around the Clock," 1953, by Jimmy DeKnight and Max Freedman)—later on, Liverpool, England (the Beatles, first heard here in 1964)—rock might be thought of as citified rural music. "Rock around the Clock," for example, imitates country style, typically in its use of the three basic chords of tonic harmony (labelled "I", "IV", and "V"):

Rock Around The Clock

Max C. Freedman & Jimmy DeKnight

Put your glad rags on and join me Hon' we'll have some fun when the clock strikes 1 We're gonna Rock A - round The Clock Tonight we're gonna Rock Rock Rock 'til broad day light we're gonna Rock gonna Rock Around The Clock Tonight

In any case, it soon had a second growth called "country rock" and an exponent named Elvis Presley, who took sexual connotations to an overt level destined to make rock the music of social revolution in the late sixties. Lyndon Johnson's "abdication" and the assassinations of Martin Luther King and Robert Kennedy made 1968 the year of focus for that rock-accompanied upheaval that is reverberating into the 1990s.

Along the way, rock divided like a cell in mitosis, spawning everything from Motown (like R & B, a purely black style) to so-called punk and acid rock. There were also longer-lasting developments, like the combinations of folk and rock starting with Bob Dylan (first recording, 1961; later the composer of Peter, Paul and Mary's "Blowin' in the Wind"). A 1970s cult figure like Bruce Springsteen, arriving with music of elemental power and words of a new sexual sophistication only a decade after the Beatles, would soon make those four seem like innocent, cheeky teenagers.

Once again, as with jazz and ragtime, the more conservative sector of America's huge public for popular music saw in rock a force of violent change and condemned it at first as pure smut. But just as surely, rock music was destined to sweep the world in a way no other nation's entertainment art had been able to do.

Meanwhile, Americans old enough to remember the songs and jazz tunes of the thirties and forties listened to them nostalgically while their offspring rocked around the clock. To distinguish styles, the print media began referring to "jazz, pop and rock"; what had been "popular music" in general was now simply called "pop." Indeed, one of the early signs of the coming demise of communism in Eastern Europe was the youthful appetite for rock throughout the region; cultural commissars resisted at first but eventually saw it as unavoidable.

Dizzy Gillespie

Americans Out Front: John Cage's Influence

Without the slightest pretense or sham, John Cage became America's guru of avant-garde music in this period. When he mapped out his rhythmic plan for a composition on involved charts (later computer printouts), when he scored for radios tuned to different frequencies or the simultaneous playing of any forty-two LP records, when he wrote for exactly four minutes and thirty-three seconds of silence (4'33", 1952), he was consistent. Cage is an authentic visionary.

Listening to his Concerto for Prepared Piano and Orchestra (1951, Nonesuch H-71202) is either a meditative experience or a test of musical patience, depending on the listener. While composing this work, Cage made a typical revelation: "Until [1950] my music had been based on the traditional idea that you had to say something. The charts [elaborate rhythmic plans] gave me my first indication of the possibility of saying nothing." Yet when Cage's delicate keyboard plinks exude their oriental vapors, many mysterious things are said—things others weren't even thinking in the early fifties.

Thus the prepared piano (in which screws and bolts of specified sizes are placed between the strings), the "happening" (later to be called "mixed media event" or "performance art") and the use of aleatoric (pure chance) music became Cage's experimental gifts to mainstream composers here and in other countries—gifts they could transform into their own brands of musical exoticism, wit and fantasy. Certainly the freely improvised passages in scores by Germany's Karlheinz Stockhausen (for example, *Zyklus*, 1959) and Poland's Krzysztof Penderecki (*Threnody for Hiroshima*, 1960) can be listed among such transformations, but the exoticism comes out most impressively in works by the American George Crumb (b. 1929) with titles like *Vox Baleinae* ("Voice of the Whale," 1971) and *Ancient Voices of Children* (1970).

Jazz musicians also took what they could use from Cage and the avant-garde of this time, when America evolved into the world center for art experimentation. Cecil Taylor (b. 1933) was the central figure in a so-called "free jazz" movement that sought in the seventies to liberate jazz from the set forms of popular and blues melodies. What he arrived at for his piano and combo of violin, alto sax, trumpet, bass and drums can be heard in nearly an hour's improvisation on a 1979 record called *3 Phasis* (New World 303).

Terming it "a masterwork," *Village Voice* jazz critic Gary Giddens refers to the music in his liner notes as "exquisitely controlled violence." The form is a series of chaotic spasms separated by solo piano ruminations, giving a curiously wild but at times hypnotic effect. Taylor's debt may be to Cage, but it is also to Cage's teacher Henry Cowell; the sounds he punches out are really tone clusters, played with a dazzling speed Cowell would hardly have imagined.

Cecil Taylor may be said to have carried something of the avant-garde spirit into jazz, where younger artists like Wynton Marsalis today still search for ways of proceeding without repeating.

Complexity Begets Simplicity

In the decades since 1968, Americans have had to absorb the Vietnam disaster, the first presidential resignation in history and subsequent economic crisis and social unrest. Small wonder that classical music, seeming to predict it all in the sixties, has since then tended rather to look nostalgically into the past.

In one sense Copland group composers stemming from the French neoclassic quarter had been doing so all along, but the German expressionist wing faced a major searching of soul. For many, twelve-tone procedure continued, but music became more tonal; others, like Milton Babbitt (b. 1916), stood ground (as late as 1989 his Schoenbergian *Transfigured Notes* was judged unplayable by the Philadelphia Orchestra, which paid a sizable commission for it anyway).

George Rochberg's experiments with "collage" led him to intersperse extended reflections on Beethoven, Schubert and Mahler with contemporary dissonance in his later String Quartets (No. 3 in 1972, Nos. 4–6 in 1979) and orchestral works. Composition in twelve tones had been too restrictive, he admitted, though the sound world it introduced was not to be abandoned. His romantically colored references to the past, pasted between the more austere passages deriving from his Schoenberg period, had the effect of ushering in a revival of tonality as an up-to-date resource. By the early 1980s Rochberg had lost some of his prophet status but remained influential in his shift back toward romanticism. Charles Hamm wrote then (p. 578) that Rochberg's "career can serve to sum up this era in American music."

Harris group nationalism à la Bartok went somewhat out of fashion in this period, but Barber-style romanticism had a rebirth in, among other places, the operas of Dominick Argento (b. 1927), the orchestral scores of John Corigliano (b. 1938) and the obsession of David del Tredici (b. 1927) with the world of

Lewis Carroll's *Alice in Wonderland.* It may be more than coincidence that these three composers are Italian-American and that George Rochberg's neoromanticism was originally nurtured at Curtis Institute by compatriots of Puccini named Scalero, Giannini and Menotti. Barber himself, having failed to capture the audience with his opera *Antony and Cleopatra* (opening night at the new Metropolitan Opera House in 1966), became posthumously the nation's

---

Reflecting two of America's most significant social changes after World War II, women and Black composers began to receive recognition (performances, grants, professorships) rarely known to them before.

Typical of the latter group is David Baker (b. 1931), a prolific exponent of classicized jazz à la Gunther Schuller. Baker's colleague on the University of Indiana faculty, cellist Janos Starker, helped make his name known in the 1970s by performing his dynamic Cello Sonata (1974) widely. He continues to produce impressive larger-scale music as well.

Ellen Taaffe Zwilich (b. 1939), a Pulitzer Prize recipient for her Symphony No. 1 in 1983, is a skillful craftswoman who keeps as busy fulfilling commissions in the 1990s as many of her male counterparts. Her Concerto Grosso (1985), based freely on Handel's Violin Sonata in F Major, applies Rochberg-style paraphrase with a fine sense of sonority.

Nothing about the music of Baker or Zwilich now suggests the out-of-the-mainstream quality that formerly characterized the work of non-Caucasian, non-male creative musicians. American women and Black composers, as well as women and Blacks in the other arts, may soon stop being identified by race or gender.

From *Peanuts,* by Charles Schultz

composer of mourning over Vietnam when his Adagio for Strings accompanied the film *Platoon* (1986).

By the 1990s, *Antony and Cleopatra* was being successfully revived (Chicago Lyric Opera, 1991), and composers like David Diamond (b. 1915) and Howard Hanson were being reappraised. A *New York* magazine review on July 30, 1990, gave this testimony:

> Prominent among [conductor Gerard] Schwarz's choices is the once-esteemed school of American symphonists . . . who flourished between 1920 and 1950 as they earnestly developed a national symphonic idiom based on . . . European models. Schwarz plays the unfashionable music of Howard Hanson . . . whenever he can, and he has found . . . Delos Records of Los Angeles which aims to record the complete [Hanson] symphonies . . . with Schwarz conducting."

Probably the best reflection of recent trends toward romanticism is the career of William Bolcom (b. 1938). Not only jazz but the whole range of this century's pop, cabaret and band pavilion music is his well of inspiration as he continues along the path marked out by his friend Rochberg. His Piano Concerto (1976) typifies his impulsive earlier period; recent works like the Symphony No. 5 (1989) probe more deeply.

Bolcom's Symphony No. 4 (1987, New World 356-2, see pp. 56-57) opens with an eclectic movement entitled "Soundscape," which more or less sums up Sessions group concerns and implications, then dissolves into a twenty-five-minute setting of Theodore Roethke's poem, "The Rose," for soprano and orchestra. The transcendent closing words

> And I rejoiced in being what I was:
> . . . .
> And in this rose, this rose in the sea-wind,
> Rooted in stone, keeping the whole of light,
> Gathering in itself sound and silence—
> Mine and the sea-winds'

Fourth Symphony, 2nd Movement

William Bolcom

Cello and bass parts omitted.

inspire Bolcom to shift without apologies from twelve-tone melody toward the C-major world of late Prokofiev. Bolcom's full score depicting the "gently rolling" sea , followed a few pages later by his serene setting of the first line above (the voice combined with only a "clear"-sounding harp, one plucked piano bass string and four very soft French horns) demonstrates the strength of this pull toward romanticism.

Nicholas Slonimsky, the century's most colorful observer of contemporary music, speaks of Bolcom's wild experiments in "serial thematics, musical collage, sophisticated . . . plagiarism and microtonal electronics" (*Baker's Biographical*

It was the great Italian composer-pianist Ferruccio Busoni who first predicted, in his New Esthetic of Music (1907), that electronic instruments would eventually challenge the role of conventional strings, woodwinds and brass. Bringing this about technologically became a contribution of the United States—perhaps one of its most musically significant—after mid-century. Until then, only the Hammond electric organ had begun to fulfill Busoni's prophecy, appearing first budget television, where tone quality was a secondary consideration.

Soon the electronic church organ followed, then the Moog synthesizer with its far sharper imitation of instrumental timbres. The more accessible electronic keyboards, on which rock and later minimalist music depended, inevitably mushroomed. At this writing, computerized instruments (by now Japanese-made, to be sure) are leaving the synthesizer far behind, imitating even the elusive sound and touch of the piano closely enough to impress the professionals.

But the most revolutionary consequence—composition for taped sound, beginning with John Cage in the early fifties—continues in force despite the turn toward Romanticism. New works keep emerging from university electronic studios, while others, like Milton Babbitt's Vision and Prayer (1961) and A Poem in Cycles and Bells (1954) by the team of Otto Luening (b. 1900) and Vladimir Ussachefsky (b. 1911) remain classics of their kind.

One clue to the future: manufacturers' sales of strings, woodwinds and brass instruments to retailers in the United States, slumping through much of the eighties, increased in 1989 an average of 5 percent over the previous year, to $316 million.

Dictionary of Musicians, 7th ed., p. 294). In the Fourth Symphony his wildness subsides into a romantic tranquility as deliberate as if it were closing the story of *Romeo and Juliet*.

If collage and neoromanticism were gestures—intended or not—toward regaining the ear of a large audience, what Philip Glass (b. 1937) fashioned at this time out of the patterned repetitions in oriental music, on the one hand, and the electronic cutting edge of rock, on quite another, turned out to be a veritable embrace.

It came to be called minimalism, and at this writing it remains the musical phenomenon of the day—reviled by many, worshiped by more than a few. The technique of stating a commonplace phrase, then stringing together many repetitions before moving to the next phrase, leads to the creation of long, static compositions in emulation of the Indian *raga* (the basic melodic type of India; Glass actually shaped the style during frequent visits to the subcontinent). People who have never cared for opera still talk in terms of reverence for those sold-out performances of *Satyagraha* (1980), *Akhnaten* (1983), and especially *Einstein on the Beach* (1976), which Glass made with the creative writer/director Robert Wilson. Recordings of all three remain in print (CBS Records).

In recent years Glass has turned to chamber opera, basing *The Juniper Tree* (1984), *A Thousand Airplanes* (1988) and *Hydrogen Jukebox* (1990) on the same small-ensemble resources he started with in the sixties. He also uses the same melodic and harmonic patterning, continuing to depend on sudden dynamic

Philip Glass

changes and shifts of harmony for emotional effect (for example, the hushed moment in *A Thousand Airplanes* when the spacecraft's landing in New York City is described).

Perhaps it is the repeated use of such devices that brings the most criticism to minimalists like Glass, John Adams (*Nixon in China*, 1987; *The Death of Klinghoffer*, 1991) and others, but the large public for this music is holding up well. Owing much to the avant-garde experiments of earlier years, as well as to rock, minimalism is a development holding a clue to the immediate future. America's influence, it tells us, is toward simplification, clarification, communication.

Developments in popular music offer a similar clue. "Revival" is the key word—revival of what is now being called "classic" jazz and of musical comedy. (Witness the astounding authenticity of restaging in *Jerome Robbins's Broadway* and the Lincoln

---

In 1973 Richard Nixon's White House staff discovered that Eugene Ormandy's choice of Vincent Persichetti (1915–87) to write a second inaugural composition had a serious flaw—Persichetti was basing his piece on Lincoln's well-known Second Inaugural Address. Nixon's advisers, aware of Lincoln's call to "bind up the nation's wounds" and seek "a just and lasting peace among ourselves and with all nations," saw this as a form of anti-Vietnam protest. They asked that a different text be chosen; Persichetti refused. A Lincoln Address was withdrawn from the Philadelphia Orchestra's gala program and later premiered by the St. Louis Symphony (without the impact of its forerunner, Copland's A Lincoln Portrait).

Persichetti thus became the first American composer to experience overt political censorship. This dubious honor was won by a prolific worker and beloved teacher (Juilliard School) who, as a student of Roy Harris, belongs with the Harris group (note the lofty simplicity of the Third Piano Sonata of 1943 and the String Symphony No. 5 of 1954, recorded on New World No. 370).

But certainly nothing in the music or personality of so benign a composer could have threatened to make a political point. That job had to be accomplished for him more than one hundred years before, by Abraham Lincoln.

Center revivals of complete shows from *Show Boat* to *South Pacific*. We've had revivals even of Victor Herbert operettas and nostalgic looks backward at Dick Powell movies (*Dames at Sea*, 1968) and London revues (*Oh! Coward*, 1972).

American composers in the nineties will most likely continue their search for ways in which to revive tonality, rhythmic simplicity and the other features that made music of the past accessible. Yet they will probably not surrender altogether the innovational elements through which recent music became relevant to twentieth-century life.

Seen from the close of the twentieth century, the most significant symbol of the good health of American music is its reversal of the flow of influence across the Atlantic.

At the same time, new lines of influence are being strung and reinforced between America and the Orient. A certain characteristic openness has not only made America a musical haven for Asians, but has led John Cage, Philip Glass and others to base their innovations on music from the East.

Of the four classical groups emerging through this eventful century, the Copland can be said to remain influential with a large public and the Barber to be regaining lost ground. Sessions group music continues to send its vibrations back to Europe, though it has lost the dominance it once had over the domestic concert scene.

Only the Harris group, with its mood of austerity and prairie pride, seems to have missed making a full impact. Perhaps the tendency of its broad singing lines to turn up more appealingly in Copland group music has robbed it of staying power.

Even if none of the innovations mentioned above—Schuller's "third stream," Rochberg's "collage," Glass's "minimalism"—turns out to be a wave of the future, they were American originals as surely as the ideas of Stravinsky and Schoenberg were European. The time when an Edward MacDowell could take his lead from the continent and a Charles Ives could eccentrically reject the same influence had long since passed.

After a century during which classical composers remained largely estranged from their listening public while American popular music spread to the entire world, American musicians have led the way in restoring tonality as a legitimate classical resource. The result has been greater musical interplay and comprehension.

In an ideal society, music both popular and classical would be intelligible, or at least acceptable, to a populace ever ready to improve its understanding of the art that may be the most complex but is decidedly the most emotionally palpable of all. American society is surely less than ideal. But its relationship to the music created here of late offers hope that the twenty-first century may see it moving toward an ever more perfect union of openness, diversity and excellence.

Atonal. Lacking a tonal center, as opposed to "tonal," or centered around a particular *scale* tone. Melodies are said to be atonal if they do not gravitate toward a center tone, or "do" of the standard "do-re-mi" scale. Harmonies are similarly atonal if they do not gravitate toward a *triad* built on a "do" or keynote of a *scale*. There are various degrees of tonal centering; music is generally labeled atonal only when it clearly has no central tone.

Cacophony. Discordant, or bad, sound (from Greek *kakos*, bad).

Chromatic (from Greek *chroma*, color). Using half-step progression (the black as well as the white keys of the keyboard) rather than some combination of half steps and whole steps as in the "do-re-mi" *scale*. Melodies are chromatic when they emphasize half step movement, harmonies when based on such movement. The result can be an unstable sliding effect or a greater intensity of feeling.

Consonance. The quality of sounding agreeable together. Consonant harmony is based on the pairing of tones that blend rather than clash, namely thirds and sixths (in the "do-re-mi" *scale*, the sounding of the third or sixth scale tone with the keynote of the scale).

Dissonance. The quality of clashing rather than blending in sound. Dissonant harmony is based on the pairing of tones that clash, namely seconds and sevenths (that is, in the "do-re-mi" scale, the sounding of the second or seventh scale tone with the keynote of the scale).

Dodecaphonic. See *Twelve-tone*.

Expressionism. The name given to twentieth-century German art, afterwards also to music, that contrasts with French impressionism by seeking self-expression rather than registering impressions of the external world. Developing just before World War I in the *atonal* music of Schoenberg, it was given a less extreme but still *dissonant* and hard-edged sound by Hindemith and Alban Berg after the war.

Fugue (fuge). Musical form in which a theme is stated in one "voice" or part and imitated in successive others according to rules of varying degrees of strictness.

Harmony. The musical result when a chord, formed by sounding at least three tones together (or implied by sounding two) moves to other chords according to certain rules. History indicates that before the Middle Ages harmony did not exist; all the music that has survived from that time is single-line melody.

Half step. The shortest distance between tones in conventional Western music. On the keyboard, the seven white and five black keys of an *octave* provide the most graphic illustration of our twelve half steps. The music of India, North Africa and other non-Western cultures may use far more divisions of the *octave*.

Major. Term describing the *mode* employing the "do-re-mi" *scale* as its source of melody and *harmony*.

Minor. Term describing the *mode*, darker in color than the *major mode*, employing the "do-re- mi" *scale* with "flatted" third and sixth tones (that is, these tones are lowered by a *half step).*

Mode. As in the world of fashion or other usage, where it means "manner" or "style," in music mode means a particular set of basic elements—melodic, harmonic, or rhythmic—that fix the general mood of a work. Before the seventeenth century, modes were more numerous and subtly differentiated than the simple *major-minor* duality that has dominated Western music since then.

Monophonic, polyphonic. Literally, having one or having many sounds (that is, voices or parts). Music is monophonic (as used herein) if a single voice dominates other secondary voices, polyphonic if no voice is more important than another. The clearest example of monophony in this sense would be a melody sung with or without chord accompaniment; of polyphony, a simple round or a Bach *fugue*.

Neobaroque, neoclassic, neoromantic. Terms referring to twentieth-century styles based on one of the three main periods in Western music: baroque (1600–1750, the time of Monteverdi, Handel and Bach); classical (1750–1820, the time of Haydn, Mozart and Beethoven); and romantic (1820–1900, the time of Schumann, Mendelssohn, Wagner and Brahms). In each case the "neo-" style interprets its model in a modern context, with judicious use of *dissonance,* rhythmic innovation and melodic freedom.

Octave. The musical distance between a tone and the nearest one with a duplicating sound, so-called because this phenomenon occurs in the "do-re-mi" scale on the eighth tone (*octo* is Latin for "eight") above or below a given "do."

Polyphonic. See *Monophonic.*

Postromantic, postexpressionist. These terms describe twentieth-century styles that carried major movements to a different level or degree of intensity, while preserving—unlike "*neo-*" movements—their basic characteristics. Mahler is the definitive postromantic, in the sense that he inherited directly and expanded a preceding style.

Scale. Stepwise succession of tones within the *octave,* forming the raw material out of which melodies and harmonies are made. Some types of scales are: diatonic (or "do-re-mi" *major* and *minor*), pentatonic (five- note), alternating (whole eps and half steps in alternation), chromatic (all half steps), wholetone (all whole steps).

Semitone. Synonym for *half step*.

Serial. The term applied to *expressionist* music in which melodies are constructed out of a "series" of tones that take the role played by a *scale* or *mode* in traditional music. The most common series is built by sounding the twelve tones in progression, without repetition of any tone, so as to avoid most effectively the feeling of tonal center.

Syncopation. Musical rhythm normally falls into groups of two or three equal beats, the first of which is accented or emphasized. Syncopation is shifting the accent to a normally weaker beat, or to an interval between beats.

Tonal. See *Atonal*.

Triad. Chord built with the first, third and fifth tones of a *scale*. The progression from one actual or implied triad to another, according to certain rules, forms what is called triadic *harmony*.

Twelve-tone. Based melodically or harmonically on a scale using all twelve tones (black *and* white keys) of an *octave*. The term "twelve-tone music" is generally used to describe the style, pioneered by Arnold Schoenberg, in which the traditional pull toward a "key" note or chord as point of repose is deliberately avoided. Melodies are made to accomplish this through *serial* techniques; harmonies are formed without concern for traditional relations between *consonance* and *dissonance*

The author and the publisher would like to extend their gratitude for permission to reproduce illustrations and musical passages from the following:

Christy's Minstrels, Song Book cover (n.d.) Drawn by Sarony, printed by Sarony & Major, Museum of the City of New York, 29.100.869A. The J. Clarence Davies Collection

Photo of Mr. and Mrs. Charles Ives, from the Charles Ives papers in the Music Library of Yale University, New Haven, Conn. Used with permission.

"Make Believe," from *Show Boat,* lyrics by Oscar Hammerstein II, music by Jerome Kern. ©1927 PolyGram International Publishing, Inc. (1416 North La Brea Avenue, Los Angeles, CA 90028. Copyright renewed. International copyright secured. All rights reserved.

"Why Should I Care?" Cole Porter. ©1937, Chappell & Co. (renewed). All rights reserved. Used by permission.

"Silk Stockings," Cole Porter. ©1955, Chappell & Co. (renewed). All rights reserved. Used by permission.

Partch instruments from Partch, *Genesis of a Music,* 2nd edition. New York: Da Capo Press, 1974. Used by permission.

A Lincoln Portrait. ©1943 by Aaron Copland; copyright renewed. Reprinted by permission of the Estate of Aaron Copland, copyright owner, and Boosey & Hawkes, Inc., sole licensee.

Piano Fantasy. ©1957 by Aaron Copland; copyright renewed. Reprinted by permission of the estate of Aaron Copland, copyright owner, and Boosey & Hawkes, Inc., sole licensee.

Photo of Robert Palmer and Aaron Copland, courtesy of Robert Palmer.

Third Symphony, Roy Harris. ©1939 (renewed) G. Schirmer, Inc. International copyright secured. All rights reserved. Used by permission.